ReCreation

An Anthology of Poetry and short Fiction

Kanyampa Manda

authorHOUSE®

AuthorHouse™ UK
1663 Liberty Drive
Bloomington, IN 47403 USA
www.authorhouse.co.uk
Phone: 0800.197.4150

Published by AuthorHouse   02/27/2019

ISBN: 978-1-7283-8416-0 (sc)
ISBN: 978-1-7283-8420-7 (e)

Dedication

For my wife Elizabeth and my children Kameko, Kalenga, and Kanyampa ,

Gratitude to Wilson Tembo, Henry Mingochi and Rose Kalwani for believing in the project.

ReCreation;

to rebrand, to exact specifications.

to amuse, to make time; to secure the leading girl back to school

to light the way, to ensure warmth to the forgotten kids of the street,

to ease the broken hearts of want,

to tender the mad off the naked street of dirt,

to get to seventh street.

To the amusement park, parcel;

Linguistic abracadabra; suggestions of gist,

Insight, foresight into the humanity tangram, damaged relationships darn.

Positioning to remodel the world making it more habitable,

Warranting, not just food security, but, a fullness in mind, body and soul.

We will remake the world.

ReCreation,

Table of Contents

Thyself-
Love thyself
    to appreciate,
        love
to love
thy neighbour-
-Thy kingdom.

1992
Kitwe

1. Perfection Creation

There she reared, whole
and well defined,
like a bird atop a high tree.
Chirrup, tweet!
Songs, oh melodies so sweet,
so, so full of justification-life.

We all gave a nod
and bid hats off to the warden.
And smirk about his sculpture,
a clear depiction,
of a girlish archetype,
a
Perfection Creation.

12/07/82
For Chola Mumbi, Lusaka.

2. **Sonantine**

Let thy Cupid's arrow inflamed direct

Take upon Apollo's moon walk.

Traverse land and sea,

And in the valleys of abundance,

The fairest creature pierce and behold.

Beside the rivers of love to rest.

In valance, rich maternity.

Thy valley's girl desires

A bounty-trappings, shopping.

In majestic red-gold and green

Soothe valerian calm,

Ex gratia in thy maiden's hand,

Votary upon the heart's fire

And true heaths restore.

Sonantine.

The Power of Love

Love is the tonic
that gives life, health, and vigour.
And to be loved is the epitome
that gives the swarm, the pride of lions
the dream of living.

A woman in love is a devil,
like a witch's cauldron astir.
And love not returned
is as tinder dry to set ablaze
a conflagration to consume her very being.

A man in love is a simpleton,
like a child to sit on fire.
And love not returned
is like watching a movie to wake up to reality.
Romeo and Juliet transform.

Love is the light that glosses the stars,
that irradiates her face in a halo,
a forge that moulds the strength
that powers a man
to heights, higher and higher.

Love paves and lights the way;
love sings the songs of life.
Come, let's make love;
let's fly up high, embrace the stars,
and shoot the moon.

The power of love.

4. **These Young Lovers**

They walk the roller skates
up and about the coin of vantage,
their reality a roller coaster.
Down the street they go strut, hand in hand
                         in a court of arms.
They ride the motorcade of panoramic splendour,
their carnival street in total flank
of cavalry armour and a don of paparazzi
in royal installations back in ham palace.
                    Back, back in ham palace.
They are the birds of the air,
knowing neither lobour nor toil;
they sing the song of the fairies
and eat the bread of sweet togetherness;
                    they eat the bread of life.
They sing the rivers of fantasy;
they lord the sea, two thousand leagues.
Like the Robin Hood of old they quest, they venture,
a portrait of paragon in a vanity case, a trail,
                    bank-rolling the children of want.
They chart glasnost and perestroika,
and blow up the foul winds
to capitals round the globe,
to champion the good of the cause;
                    they blaze the trail.
They are the dreams come true,
and if we raise
our consciences high, they are the means,

the will, the free spirit,
                    the power to make a change.
These young lovers.

10/02/98
Ammanyao

5. **This Poetry**

Holding it
like a small blank piece of paper,
reading through it
with the tip of my pen
leaving marks behind ...
      standing,
            slanting, and
         circling ...
      all shapes and fancy.
   Yes!
A perfect creation
forming and disappearing
at the back of my mind
as this piece of paper
can no longer hold any ink.

I read through it,
this piece of poetry,
and surely it turned out to be you ...
Ruth!
Do you think about me?
I always do and wonder...
When will reality dawn,
when and when?
Definitely let it not be before
the close of this poetry;
      let it be,
         let it be you, and only

let it be me;
send your love to me,
and let this poetry
dawn the sunshine of love.

09/08/82
Unza, Lusaka.

6. Eyes of Choice

My eyes of choice,
    my mind of dirty,
        drive me
            deep and trouble
          shaky waters in the midst;
        sweet and flowers surpass.
    Oh, my eyes of gold,
rescue me.

29/01/85
Kalulushi.

Eyes Tell no Lies

Eyes spoke to eyes
of warmth and fondness of love
of attraction and desire.

Eyes spoke to eyes
the fiery anger of vermin
to fierce eruptions.

How could eyes bedevil
when the sport of the eye
dilates with a message in a nimbus.

How could eyes lie
when the pupils narrowed to pinpoints
surely spoke what the lips dared not.

How could eyes deceive
when you fix your optic
and slaps! dead in our tracks.

Indeed, eyes spoke.
How could eyes be wrong
when the lachrymose-red in a mirage
pleaded for understanding?

For niece Pamela Mwape N.
07/08/97

8. Grace

Is thy name,
thy kingdom?
We dwelleth with a new hope
        every day.
Lady of sweet and high degree,
a promise to the hand that giveth
sure a distant star.
An oasis trailing thirty days journeying.
We open eyes
        To kisses, to wine,
        to wisdom's delight;
        our eyes we turn.
The delight of creation
To kisses to wine
To wisdom delight
Our eyes we open;
Thy love,
        starlight,
            Thyself,
                sure existence.
Airs and graces.
Shall I eternally employ
the mighty and glory of Jah love?
The promise ...
        Imanity's perpetual vision,
        the call, the frontline.
        Long may he bloom
        and thaw steadily.

       For surely
Grace
       is thy name,
          thy kingdom.
With a new hope, we dwelleth.

07/08/85
At Kalulushi, for G. M.
May her soul continue to reside in God's grace.

9. **Elaiza**

I read the classics
and trail Odysseus
to the long high seas,
to the siege of Troy.

I sing the wailers uprising,
the Rastaman chant,
hail Igziabeher,
and fly away home to Zion.

I eat the giants of Gulliver's
and the white sperm-whale Moby Dick.
I scrape the snows of Kilimanjaro
and revisit the lord of the flies.

I walk in the night,
deep in the heart of the matter,
right through creation.
I stalk, I search.

I champion the shooting star
and stop at the Southern Cross.
I take aim at the moon.
Shine on yellow bloom.

I tap the wine of Galilee,
and the oasis of savvy

and heavens come down
upon my eyes; open the Copernicus.

I drink the waters of love
down the waterfront
and stand sentinel over my labour of love
to the everlasting nectar.

I call the name
for whom the bell knells;
like the call of the wild,
a reverberating report in balladary composition.

Each and every day, millions of years transform
in my waking and in my rest.
I fill up only with you,
the portrait of my affection.

Each and every night, I count the stars.
I traverse the Milky Way
and cry tears to fill,
to fishes' delight

I ask more questions than answers get,
in these fields of gold.
I am the pearl diver.
I reach out for gold.

I ride in flight's romance.
I am the fish eagle

up in a twenty-one MiG's display
for the only fish in the sea.

I hail Igziabeher
for this gift in a princess suite,
this kiss of life.
Elaiza.

July, 1997, for wife, Elizabeth
Mogoditshane, Botswana.

10. Angelina

Oh come,
    oh rain,
    come seasons we play
    in torrents; angel delight.
our troubled souls, touch
our scorched backs, soothe
our desultory walk, shape.
Oh come,
    oh rain,
    come seasons we play
in torrents, Angelina Benedictine,
    our molten brains cool
    and charter our intellectual train acourse;
    we recline in a tortured slumber,
our hearts in our mouths,
our heads in our arms.
We rave, we a rapid dogs;
we shout in a call of the wild,
we scream a crickets' sing-song.
Oh come,
    oh rain,
    come seasons we play
in torrents, Angelina Benedictine,
    our shacks and mansions,
    heaths and bakeries transform
    our living rooms, desert sands,
    our beds seas of saline.

Oh come,
   oh rain,
   come seasons we play,
Angelina.

07/11/96 To Mr. Moremong
for Montsamaisa and Angelina.

11. Tshala Muana

She sings
with the passion and immersion
of a person gripped,
held in trust by thousands of
vocal devils;
she realizes the scriptures.

She struts the stage
with the pride of a lion,
roaring his mane, his pride,
churning out soul-searching ambiances
to the delight and security the cub sing.

She reaches out, man to woman,
soul to soul,
spell casting, spellbound,
like the hogs of the book
go crushing the multitudes of melody courtesans.

She is Tshala, babes,
living up to the sapient tidings
of leisure culture and the Zairean beat;
she's the greatest of them all.
She's the Tina Turner of Africa; she is

Tshala Muana.

26/01/92
Ammanyao.

12. On Your Wedding Day

When the sun shall down come,
down the horizon
in osculation enduring,
we shall turn low the lights, and
let nature take its course.

The moon shall up come,
up high the courts of heaven,
giving the brace the glow of love;
the wedding bells shall sound,
and the old man in the name most revered
shall proclaim-man and woman.

The wine the men shall toss,
the cake the women shall taste,
the merry-go-round, the children shall ride.
and in chorus, all shall join in
celebration, ululation, and jubilation
for the day pronounce celestial.

True love extolled,
the knot thus tied in grace.
For better for worse,
in glass halls and dungeons,
we shall turn the lights down low,
and let nature take its course.

The sun shall touch the horizon
in osculation enduring;
the moon shall up come,
up high the courts of heaven,
giving the brace the glow of love,
the cradle of perpetual elation

On your wedding day.

07/07/83,
Unza Library, Lusaka.
For Mbamu, ba Roomie.

13. Child In Tyme

Blessed be, thy little one,
blessed be, thy
child in tyme.

I welcome you,
my child,
child my own.

How can I show
how happy am I?

Blessed be, thy
sweet little dear.

Take the light, the stars,

the joys, your father, the mind peaceful and loving;
take my mind, my own.

I love you, my dear little angel.
Be the meaning to my life,
my happiness, my love, my treasure.

And grow big and strong
with a mind and brain
and a heart huge and warm.

Such as will love,
such as will entreat,
and star and show the way.

Take this love, dear child so sweet,
from me all my desire.
Welcome, little lovely one,

Child in tyme.

15/02/83
For Happy Chisulo's firstborn.

14. **Daughters Of Bourgeois**

There they walk, rancid,
daughters of the bourgeois, one tyme
faces down; down cast,
and seas shine in their eyes
and leaks drip under their roof
if you met them only today
they are faces at crossroads

They are faces at crossroads
the reflection in their main
neither of fish nor crustacean
the bloom in their tree
not of the spring
but of the fall, fall, fall fold

But of the fall, fall, fall, fold
by the show of presence
living way beyond the sea!
and pencil boxes full
automated by an array of machinists
neither a care nor toil
now they cry, now they curse

Now they cry, now they curse
of a generation of waste
now they see, now they hail labour dignity
and a vision for posterity
they charter their intellectual course

they put the seed in
and living flowers upon mothers' grave shine.

30/03/83
In the staffroom at Mufulira Secondary School.
Grace Bwalya was there.

15. **COUNT YOUR BLESIINGS**

We blame and curse
only when you've seen it all
trials like you've never known,
Count yourself lucky.

We sulk and grieve
only when you've known disaster
troubles like you'd never decipher
count yourself amongst them.

We rave and blubber
only when you've witnessed the crash of the Titans
the clash of Iron, of lead of blood
count your stars.

We sing and shout
only we haven't known the music,
the vision in tune ...
count your blessings.

COUNT YOUR BLESIINGS

27/07/97
For Speech Day, Mpelembe Secondary School,

kitwe.

16. **Hyenas Wait Our Table**

We left our senses trite
cultured and of civil invite
the salt and water of discretion
the spirit and constitution

We littered our way
tainted all the way
the seed of discord so we sowed
of harvests dread deny

We left our own
in pursuit God knows, what!
to women less the name
to purposes on ego trip
to a bed of shame

We took women forsake
of the streets so to speak
the lamp under the brush
of salt iodate devoid
and hyenas wait our table

Sins of youth in dignified sage
to worst crimes of wedlock
and supper ego deny
to sanity cast overboard
we took leave

We dwell this earth we walk
we take charge so to speak
to rule over large and small
yet the road, the most trodden we bus
to a bed of shame

20/7/97
Ammanyao.

17. **Soul Search**

The only mind retain
a grubby one;
Years of dodgem transfiguration
took their toll.
With the soul patently counted out
hovering somewhere, maybe in purgatory
in valleys deep down low!
And the heart filthily calculating
like a cat moving on to a canary
with the callousness only of a German
Submarine captain on combat duty
never to vulgarise native soil
in this investment in a Bulls and Bears
enterprise
the only mind, a sullied mind.

The asceticism of denial no longer holds
trading illicit words with relish
self-fulfilment now the ritual
the angels of miracles no longer the
knight in shining armour
as restraint is cast utopia wise In these places of
psychedelics,
where we yak in sweet abandon!
Young, old and aged
friends and friends of our friends,
and release! Down to the basic humanity
like an avenging angel of the apocalypse

the only mind, oh so, so grubby,
In this search within ...

SOUL SEARCH.

14/11/96
Title by Mkandatsama, D. lovemore.
a Zimbabwean friend.

Mogoditshane, Botswana.

18. Night

I cry out, to reach out to you
my immortal friend.
I have no serenity, I can't wait
to embrace you my ...
my salvation
my only rest,
night my friend ...
rescue me.

Yet, as I rest my head
to clinch you,
my cold bed,
my rock pillow,
The tap, tap of my shoes
repeats in my subconscious,
one two, one two
Three, four, one two
follow, follow. Follow!

A legion of soldiers, marching
in my head
Hammering away at the earth,
consuming my energy,
Counting down my years,
trailing me to the battle front,
The front line.
Whose battle am I fronting?

Up again in this jungle against my constitution
my feet, my only transportation
my thoughts I stand at a distance!
one two, one two, Three, four, one two
never, ever reprieve
one two, one two
night my immortal friend
rescue me.

12/07/89
For Nawa Machwani, one of the travellers.

19. ONE LOVE

For the forgotten kids of the street
Craving warmth on a breezing night
And morsels of bread wafting off their table
To sniffing concoctions of obscenities, so they shelter.

All I ask,

A cane to forestall the degrading means of locomotion,
To secure the leading girl back to school,
to lead the blind back home.

All I desire,

An escalator
To raise the lame up the stirs
To ease the broken hearts of want.

All I hanker

A nurse to tender the mad
Off the naked streets of dirt and garbage pan,
Safely to the asylum.

Yes, if I had one wish, one love,
Why!
A herbal potent
Beyond the ills of our times,

ONE LOVE, ONE HEART, ONE IMANITY.
2007,03.

20. **Silences**

It's not a silent hurt we have
not a blind I
not a blank here
perfect bright visions we have;
our ears to the grass;
this land, quiet steel! so

This land, quiet steel! so
like a running stream at 2 am
in the rest of night
no!
It's not a silent hurt we have ear,
and thieve break locks at 2 O'clock.

The yarn is obvious
this poetry clearer steel!
the silence even more weighty,
mamas, papas,
and children alike; all
all silent

All silent
only but, the brood, who know no limits
mutter and urge
mama, mama
po..or..ri..dge
and the world looks on ...

silent steel!
and thieves break locks at 2 O'clock

Even to a splash of dirt
on to our Sunday best,
we amble on,
to a flash at full beam in the I
from the big boy, Mr. super boss
silences

Yet one thing be sure
the iceberg, only the tip
and when the sea seems so tranquil
the heaviest burdens ease
and thieves break locks at 2 am
they've robbed the supermarket
in a daylight swoop
S i l e n c e s.

1993
UNZA, Lusaka.

21. **Protect And Guide**

In the valley
deep in the heart of the dell
we hurt so much
only thy deliverance,
protect and guide I and I

The birds of emancipation
flying up high;
now owls
heralding death everyday
only thy deliverance
protect and guide I and I

The poor man in the midst of plenty
oh, no money to spend, no food to eat
the children's outstretched hands receive not
they cry in the night, poor boys and girls
no place to rest I and I head
only thy deliverance
protect and guide I and I

In this gorge of deep-felt confusion
deep down Oh!
we're about to be submerged
totally and finally
swimming in the valley of deep-felt sleaze
our birds of liberty
grabbing the last loaf from poor mother

The children's outstretched hand
receive not, they cry,
we wait upon thy grace
we wait upon thy table of grace
only thy deliverance
protect and guide I and I

Our material guides, flying our ideals up there
now locusts devouring all green, erasing our
humanity
our court of arms, our strength, owls, heralding
death everyday ...
only thy love, only, only thy mighty might
only thy deliverance Jah, Jah,
protect and guide I and I Rastafarai

5/10/84

22. **The Rolling Stones**

Some stones roll
and gather no moss,
others roll and gather all
     of drudgery and utter indigence
     we a dung beetles
     in a humble acceptance
of clout and toxicity
they a buoyant shooting stars
in a winner takes all
     we roll on,
     in a lunar whirl commune
     in a endless search for the proverbial
     needle
they glide on
in a legato skates skilfully
in a endless sun showers
     we trudge on
     a rich past to mail home
     and a name for posterity
they charter on
to feasts of merry, to nobility invite
and a legacy for inheritance.
     Yet opportunities proliferate,
     in fields of fury
     and the American dream!
Stop! Hold on to the stone
charter the plane

and gather all.
THE ROLLING STONES.

*For me, 06/09/96, in the Diaspora
at Montasamaisa – Botswana.*

23. **Friends And Foes**

Life is a measure of garbage
Try it, open it!
It gravitates a reek of incidence -
of friends and foes

You wonder, you ponder
what about justice?
Out of ten denied
where lie our manger in divine?
Good intentions bolt

Acquaintances try to dispute the claim
but how far they go
only serves to save
the integrity of the whole
only, but a marriage of inconvenience

And foes go to town
and seize the law houses
and act the law, the spirit go begging!
and justice
out of ten denied.

Yet the turnaround, 365 times,
soon come
and the game of hide and seek give;
the scavengers spill the beans
and open and septic the wounds

We shall rise and wash our faces
having uncovered life's lies

Skeletons stand!
the stench of incidence
of Western democracy!
friends and foes.

07/04/87

24. **Out Of Control**

I want to be
what I like to be
I appoint to live
what I yearn to live
I long to feel
what I must feed;

Yet the more I want
the more I can't,
the further I live
no moment of truth
the more I feel
out of control.

This freedom I crave
no freedom at all,
the labours I engage,
only toils report
and frustrations chronicle
a litany of unpalatables

The games I play
only hide and seek
the wishes I dream, no horses at all
the skies I long, airs transform
this life I live
out of control.

Yes I have to be
what I want to be to labour
engage, in horizons of sunsets.
let me feel
what I want to live
out of control.
01/03/94
Kitwe
for me.

25. THEY CRY CROCHODILE TEARS

They come in all shapes and sizes,
Colours and shades
These wolves in sheep's clothing.
But their character and resolve is evident-
Selfish and selfish interest only.
Their capacity for brewing up trouble-historical,
As is evidenced in the Biblical Garden.
Their determination to deceive and preserve
their self and kind-paramount ...
Oftentimes in the guise of peace, love and care-
Through community initiatives and
blood cancer plate transfusions.
Not far-fetched if you cared to note ...
Take note, Zambia
The public platform is their craze,
they go strut the catwalk.
The innocent, the deprived, the meek, their theatre
Flushing out smiles-very plastic.
Killing and smiling Leopardesses, out
sprinting and depleting the game.
Their motivation to perpetuate
their stay in the limelight-
Increasingly become the proverbial
power corrupts ...
They slowly but surely drive their better
halves into the deep, to sure death:
ONE, for the supreme prize lost in the Middle East,
TWO, for the contest lost in Paris,

THREE, for the big game lost in London ...
America, Russia and England too!
Knowing how spent we get, they kicked
their backs and urged them on
Slave masters, Puppet lordesses
They fed them words to state and drugged them
to the civic house to make pronouncements
Just to keep the flags flying at their sides.
They cry crocodile tears out of public house
Round the boondocks, carrying the
remainders of their game
In flashy western mourning garbs
to the showgrounds,
A wardrobe for the public to fund.
Did they love! do they care!
Beware,
They come in all
shapes and sizes,
Colours and shades
These wolves
in sheep's clothing,
THEY CRY CROCODILE TEARS.

26. Survive & Prevail

The uncertainties of this tyme
like a tightening knot in me stomach
slides me sickeningly
gnawing me like forty days hunger
in the face of the prospect and
consequences
of failure
The waves of panic
rise up in some dark spot somewhere
in me soul
leaving a constant goose veneer
on me hide.

The speculations of this waiting
hangs tons upon tons of heavy weights
on me shoulder
me profile in a constant fisherman's gnarl
in this mystery and horror movie
where resolution is solely the author's key
a sense of despondency and weariness
like a dull ache in me marrow enroot
as moles bore the sinews in me limb
me walk in desultory.

The unpredictability of this condition
like a farmer in Draughterwar Somalia
unnerves me shake to
"straws of the camel's back"

In this promise of impending disaster
anvils of cars come crushing down
upon me
Under me feet, the sterility of the baking
Kgalagadi sands
Crippling and destroying me dream
the fuel upon which me run
all these years

Yet I me hold up
like a snake me cast the last vestige
of panic
of failure
of despondency
of sterility
to stand the charge of the Green Buffalo
and take me chance man to man
steel to steel as a duty
to survive and prevail
and walk like a man.

04/01/97
For Monica Wanjiku Wakenya Wakahiga-
Manda Kanyampa
Montsamaissa Private Secondary School, Botswana.

27. Dreams Come True

The silent guest
to every mind
In the shadow and In the rainbow
to minds local and minds profound
the belles and jesters at court
all, all reside
dreams come true

Ride the horses
of the riches beggars ballade
corsair the wind,
dog the seas
chatter the plane of gold
sail the dreamboat and the proverbial check
of the fowls of the dump heap.

The silent guest
to anxiety and stories about home
in foreign lands
the toots and the heralds of success stories
the gold, the silver and even the bronze
and a cultivation of Olympian detachment

The Alpha and the Omega
of present love affairs
the moon and the stars
and the sands of veracity, and prophetic refund
the silent reality ...
dreams come true.

08/10/96

28. **Time, Dreams And Days.**

Times,
architects of dreams and days,
in masonry,
in glass,
in pole and mortar.

Dreams,
visions in a mirage
moving laity and parsonage
through times blue
and skies clear
in a balance of loads and weights.

Days,
levels of conscience,
amphitheatres of trials and verdicts
the stakes and state of affairs
of verity and falsity in equal measure.

Time, Dreams and Days
pathways
stairway,
to purposes high and low
to revelations,

TIME DREAMS AND DAYS.

November 1997,
Kitwe.

For Radio Ichengelo.

29. Visions And Recollections

Just beyond the eye,
if you wish to seek the truth,
lie deeper understanding.
Yet the tunnels be long and yet interminable
in concentric circles
round and round the message goes
into layers of the past
and current manifestation
unfolding the future

Close your eyes and see
if you endeavour to behold the meaning
a head search into revelations
unveils the veneer of cogitation
a souvenir of countless successes and failures
in visions and recollections
a vista of bygone times
with nostalgic refund
an array of expectations and prospects
Lord forbid.

The details lost in the clouds, there on nine
and the destruction of self-deception recede
the spirit defused by tradition and coercion
lie naked before you
in tunnels just beyond the eye
so, so long and interminable
in circles concentric

round and round this Carousel the message goes
close your eyes and see ...

VISIONS AND RECOLLECTIONS

05/09/96

30. THIS MIND OUR MAIN

A construct
of suggestions upon associations
of experience and practice
of mind body and soul

This mind our kernel
our essence, our direction
Our discretion.

Left open and relaxed
in mortal copulation engage
so conceive and nurture a realization
to ideas and dears

We feel the pulse of the veins
we reflect in direct engagement
and project the future, oh, do we!
we count the stars.

This mind our foremost
the excavator and crane
the wonder and bloom
the gloom and marvel

A construct sure of associations
a conceiver and nurture

the reflection and projection
of the world we reside

THIS MIND OUR JUDGEMENT

02/12/97

WHISPERING WINDS AND SANDS OF TIME

The whispering winds and sands of time
storm the footpaths and passage ways of Mogoditshane
in this wintry cold dusty July weather
I know the time is done, older yet!
By the measure of the whirl of the sand
the whispering winds and sands of time.

They knock at your vestry door
they bring you face to face with yourself
and reconcile you matter of factly
deep down you hear the voice of heaven
in the whirl of the sand
The whispering winds and sands of time

The whispering winds and sands of time
cold and ashen
they whine and whip you to submission
you run on home to the rest
as the year wears by the measure
of the whirl of the sand
the whispering winds and sands of time.

Yes, on home to the rest
bridging times unflinching rigors
to songs delight everlasting reunion
to the sun and moon in perpetual canoodle
in the magic whirl of the Mosi-O-Tunya sky
the bold African violets abloom, the,

WHISPERING WINDS AND SANDS OF TIME

24/07/96
at Montsamaisa, Botswana
And for the memory of Mrs Asumani, HOD Languuages
MCM Nkana School Kitwe, October 2018.

TEN YEARS AFTER

The resolve of knowledge
The spirit of tenacity
So define.
The campus of sound judgement
The journey to a destination true
So, so relate.
The determination to achieve
The course of inde-fa-tiga-bility
So, so, so desire.

Founded on steadfastness
The stone the builders refused
The foundation stand the taste of time
Devoid of bias
Fear, free and firm
Informed by a world vision
Oblivious of a chance to break
Family, friendships
And acquaintances.

On the alert ad- infinitum
Windows of shopping change
Sidestepping to a new renaissance
To the four winds
Taking anchors of gold
Taking not butterflies that shine and fade
No! no shooting stars
Of dreams beggars ride

Embracing bees of the brews of sweet promise.

A defined, determined quality
The resolve of knowledge
The spirit of tenacity
The campus of sound judgement
The journey to a destination true
The determination to achieve
The course of indie-fa-tiga-bility
The stone the builders refused

TEN YEARS AFTER.

For Maureen Sakala
Her Farewell
06-12-18

32. The Sojourn

I hear the voice
of crickets and fireflies
singing ceaselessly,
conjuring images
like dreams come true
of movements deft and practiced
riding white horses and chariots
incessantly they sing
the crickets and fireflies

I ride the Southern Cross like the last mile
struggling to clear the edges, I
twist and turn
at the traffic circles round and round
to the magic spell of the moon at full bloom
they sing,
the crickets and fireflies
their resolve ...
a catharsis divine

I count the eggs, before they materialize
I can't wait to see them give fourth
I summon the messenger bird

the harbingers of passage
I ask the white dove to send me rice
I can't wait to taste the milk ...

on this sojourn
I ride the southern cross like the last time

20/03/96
For Kameko and Kanyampa
at Mogoditshane in Botswana.

33. A Bird In Flight

Oh how nice to be
   a bird in flight

This vast graph of a landscape
embroidered with such golden threads ...
as far as the eye could see
as long as the feeling could last.

Oh how nice to chart chariots ...
   the horses dreamers ride

And nothing to fret
than the problem of enough
crusts to eat
a ledge to shelter
on a rainy experience

Oh how nice to be
   kids on a merry go round

Riding high on this carousel
and headlong into the waters of love
and the precision,
the credit only of the fish eagle
two thousand leagues ...
   under

The freedom of a bird in flight

the laughter of the water lilies
and the dragon flies ...

Oh how nice to be
a bird in flight.

07/02/96

34. The Lone Traveller

The drum,
like a lonely soul
on lonely road
whispering out there
maybe in limbo

The message,
in mixed revelations

I sit down to muse
to wonder
only echoes stare back at me
with speaking eyes

The message still crowded
in a misty construct

Where do I go from here?
only the wind whispers back
In whirls and turns
and anxiety measure apprehension

I pick myself up
and journey on, ...
those who travel
do not look back

At Kalulushi, late 80's.

35. **The Road Is My Sheperd**

To roads high and low
I wake and bus my daily bread
from start to finish
I behold trials and tribulations.
I ride upon the Whitehorse to embrace sure the lord
of roads,
the road is my shepherd.

The road is my shepherd.
my thought, my energies, my constitution.
to my theatre company
I set my act and sit upon the forge
to get the music to the people high and low,
my effort, my working, my worship
the road is my shepherd.

The road is my shepherd
my caution and my bearing
to roads broad and narrow
to purposes nigh and taciturn, I bus
I chariots no royal roads
till the waterfront
in the deep of the roadstead
the road is my shepherd.

03/08/97
Conceived upon reading a sticker

"The Lord is My Shepherd" in a Minibus en route to Chambishi. The thought is, how serious is this considered by the minibus crew or indeed the passengers?

36. Who Will Plead For Angola

Of blood and tears
shed in vain...
to landmines maimed
to motor power deceased,
I cry for you Angola.

What a betrayal
to those that sacrificed their souls
for the liberation of their motherland
of sons and daughters
the salt and water

What a tribute
to the innocent ones that perished on the front
their reality only the cenotaph-
to the Unknown Soldier,
funeral dirges and dead flowers.

What a bleach of trust and confidence
to those that gave their whole
on the road to Uhuru
their certainly grief and anger
landmines still main, missile still ricochet

Of blood and tears
shed in vain
to landmines maimed
I cry for you Angola
Uhuru! Uhuru!

Where are the fruits
for our sweat
for our blood
for our tears
the fruit for our trust and confidence?

Speak!
Agostino Neto
talk!
Holdern Roberto
let's hear it
Jonas Savimbi.

The promise for self-determination
a revolution of hope
a yield of basic freedoms
and universal human suffrage
where is Uhuru?

What the hell is Uhuru?
Continued fighting?
Jumping from tree to tree
like gorillas we've become?
Civil war?

Now we call each other names
rebels,
insurgents,
sons against fathers

daughters up against mothers
brothers, slay brothers

Who will plead for Angola
the Cubans?
Americans?
Tanzania?
Zambia?
Ethiopia?

Elections elude us
Ten long drawn years
tears continue to crevice mothers
empty granaries
and imperialists grin at us.

Political dishonesty
political immorality
power struggle
foolish pride.
a historical test for Africa.

Of blood and tears
shed in vain
to landmines maimed
to motor power deceased
I moan for you Angola

Who will plead for Angola?

09/06/87
for Kenneth Kaunda (KK),
S Africa and Africa.

37. **Mind Body And Soul**

The clouds crackle and shatter
In faults of florescence;
this, but the harbinger.

The heavens roar
The Loins shake the foundation
all the more.

The soldiers, the garrison,
Only but instruments in
this artificial insemination.

The bulls in a stud,
In a pen;
Democracies miles on end.

The water falls
On this evening voyage
These are but ripples.

Round in a whirl, in a spin
And dying out!
The master mind retain.

The operation in the desert scene
Only a storm
In a smoke screen.

This is only but the tipsy
Foundations of stone reside
Deep down the entrails

The ridges of smoke over the Gulf stand
Only but a ricochet
To the rape of the daughters of the Holy land,

Yes by democracies
Miles and miles on end
Over lands and seas their scatter munitions, lord
report!

What Impunity lord forbid!
Denial of institutions they set to regulate
They rape the justice of the Egg.

These scorpions plague our main
The pain phenomenon,
They rock our very foundation.

We walk the glowing coals
Our souls and flesh bake
In democracies over land and sea.

There is much to mind mine
Deep down in minds oh so profound
Sardonic and crooked divine

Their purpose, set and focused
Pro..tec..tion of foreign interests in foreign lands
A façade of words possessed

Pick up axe and stone
Collected in mind, body and soul
Cut the thread, the twin chain.

MIND BODY AND SOUL.

08/04/96 Mogoditshane BOTSWANA.

BULAWAYO-
CENTRE of convergence and divergence,
Welcomes and departures
Diffusion, effusion, revision characterize
The colours of the rainbow Marimba band
Sanguine, witness, enjoin the stage.
The fowls of air chirrup,
Ballads of revelations,
Their charter from the beginning.

Son spots invite
Beauty stars the flowers,
Sunscreens deny,
Way over to dialogue
All sorts,
Dull sorts, gay sorts,
Sure sorts,
Gay garbs of manifestations, and frowns
Flowers physical and imagined
Roses, black Jacks, Hemlocks and
Especially so "Maruva enyika"

Love smiles, vanity trails
Anguish tags, dog
All invite, all all dismiss,
Beauty spots, frisky constructs, tagaties
Bees and wasps trade waves of pollen
Leaving; surely the sting
A thousand allergies cast
Two thousand leagues within

To cities and environes far and wide
Long in time and times apart.

Fire balls create, fireworks mutate
And sustenance enroute at Sis Bee's Kitchen
Shakespearean cauldrons engage
Conflagrations, promises of spirit and hope
The elephants stand vigil
The keepers of the Temple invest ...
Son spots, sunscreens
Beauty spots and tagaties
Centre of convergence and divergence.
Bulawayo.
(Maruva e nyika= Flowers of the land in Shona
language=the beautiful women.)
23/12/13 @ Bulawayo Centre and Solusi University,
Zimbawe.

THE TOWER OF STRENGTH

Sad
So sad
So bad
So shocking
So devastating
So manifestly real
And so permanent
This tower of grief
This tower of STRENGTH
This crown of thorns adorn
My eyes so sore, so sure
Dark, stars stop to shine
My tears crevasse this face
To marks of anger
To marks of anguish
My ears hear nothing
But voices of a thousand,
calling the Name to praise!
Malumbo, MALUMBO!
My mouth agape, in whispers of bewilderment
Trying to understand
My hair, in dreads of loss
Lost to meaning.
She heads the tower, that tower of grief
At the head of the tower
She stands predominant
A strong presence indeed
Faces of understanding

Careers of hope
Imprinted in words ...
With the greatest loss,
Come the greatest prize
To the care takers relief.
Dry your tears and smile
Mother and Father Face up to the sky
And say amen and AMEN.

We remember the Mwape family at the
loss of their lovely daughter, Malumbo,
in Ichibemba to mean **Praises.**

38. Freedom To Mandela

Rhythms and streams
of our nation's plenty
flowing up and yonder
like the rivers of living waters
in panoramic propensity to cherish freedom
let,
our systems transpire
in perceptive faculties
the spur of necessity
the youth, the vigour, the vista of life
into bliss in benediction
and freedom to self-determination
freedom to Mandela.
let,
the shackles
that hold our kin in servitude
in Suid Africa, in South W Africa, in Kenya!
Snap and crumble
like the greatest Victoria
sounding the drums of the African sunshine
the essence that be, our Africa.
freedom to self-determination
freedom to Mandela.
Let,
our national drums and trumpets
sound only of freedom songs
let,
the rhythms and streams

of our nation's plenty
sound only of revelations for peace
and freedom to Mandela
freedom to Ngugi.

04/03/84

39. Blessed Assurance

A grey, molten sky
the sea, the mirage
on this macadamized experience,
and then, and suddenly,
the Botswana sky weakens
and betrays the promise
the sky rumbles
shaking heaven seat
and split
and lights up in snap glows
and splashes of light
as clouds begin to collect and screen
defusing the rainbow bridge,
envisaging a natural conditioning
feeling the air aromatically
turning the Batswana on, faces aglow
and lightening and heightening
like heavens come down
Devouring mouthfuls of this promise
they chirrup like love birds
in flights of romance
and pula!
Echoes the unspoken commands
Down they go and prostrate in their nice suits
In total solidarity
and the answer!
In quadruples spoke the rain transform
like root airs on a clean shaven chin

the earth opened up the dawn of green
the promise of a new era
a blessed assurance.

30/01/96.
At the national Library
in Gaborone Botswana.

40. **Kgwanyape**

A trail of mayhemric destruction
littered her passage.
Hauling faun and fauna ...
picking the threads of the mystery
piecing them together ...
the rage of a *bereaved mother*
we all cry out, in projections of fear of uncertainty.

We all cry out, in projections of fear of uncertainty
as the day wore on
clouds collect and screen
on this, the 25th of April
with voices of lions, the heavens speak
with eyes of tigers, they gaze at unsuspecting us
Dark, grey, nightfall, forlorn

Dark, grey, nightfall, forlorn
the Vampire stalk for blood
sparkling tongues of fire, the dragon
in tentacles reaching out
dragooning peace and quiet
webbing the entire Mogoditshane
more so, D. F.

Webbing the entire Mogoditshane
the warning too late, the rains came
dogging the fiery monster in fidelity
in mountainfalls, hippos and elephants register

and quiet descends upon our reside
as thousands of tinsmiths transform our environ.

As thousands of tinsmiths transform our environ.
Animatedly committed to champion the death line
crys in the night,
man and beast alike transfix
and helplessly huddle in a corner
and hail Mary
time and age collect.

Time and age collect.

Our roofs reaped
all huddled in some corner, we cry for Mother
pointing fingers and passing the back to D.F
the whiff heavy with crimson
in this hail of flying hippos and elephants
the paws of death upon our necks,
autopsy awaits the break of dawn

Autopsy awaits the break of dawn
the blossoms all green and supple
oh! All shreds transform,
vehicles, in Dodgem transfiguration,
shock and distress descend upon us
as death reports ...
she took her revenge.

She took her revenge,

a trail of mayhemric destruction
littered her passage
hauling faun and fauna
and vehicles in Dodgem transfiguration
in this hail of flying hippos and elephants
the rage of a bereaved mother,
Kgwanyape.

NOTE: *True story-check the caption below:*

"Kgwanyape", pronounced "kwanyape", is a name of a flying snake said to have caused hailstones on the 25th April 1996, in Mogoditshane, Botswana.

The story, goes, the soldiers of the Defence Forces had picked 'baby' snakes together with some un hatched snake eggs and took them to their camp zoo.

The mother snake was very annoyed it pursued her 'children' and in the confusion of the hailstones it retrieved her own.

The destruction caused was phenomenon.

41. Song For The Witch

She's depraved
my mother's mother's sister
she's iniquitous
the very memory of infamy!

Throughout the night she talks
with people we do not see
in a language that bores the sinews in our main
sending our hairs to pedestal on end

Sometimes she smiles
often times she grins
many times she laughs the empty laughter of the
fairies
and roars the shattering of an angry lion

She rages in a show of strength
she insults in a challenge of justification and hails
her ancestry
she cries and pleads in remorse
they taunt her people in a claim of guardianship
in her binary existence

We do not see them
she surely does envisage them
the excitement in her mirth speaks enough
the horror in her eyes shines the truth

Why do you sing the night my kid sister wonders
what is so exciting about the night
why these talks in the heat of the night
what about the harmony of the night?

You smile,
you rage
you roar
and you cry

Life dear child, wait you grow and see
in pursuit of the fruits, the four winds, the two poles
no easy answers
in this origin of species

Stop it witchy woman
do not bedevil the child, the only light at the
crossroads
your revelations in our dreams more than enough
your machinations keep us gazing all night

You left us here in this shelter
to feasts of black; dreams so speak
my late pa so implores
to beware of you.

You took him away in a vampire trail; to the
underworld
said you wedded him to brides devoid of faces
that said you promised a chicken

that said you did not live up to
that said you had to offer a guzzler in its stead

On a broomstick you rode
miles and miles on end in no time
the hands of time you tempered
nights into centuries transform
hours into years past, present and future

Now you beam in nostalgic refund
now you rage, in a sure show of regret
now you roar, only you cannot effect
and now you cry, was it worth the trouble!

She's gone, celebrates the calm, the night
to this peace we urge take only
that as will cherish fresh memories
even in this origin of species
to fairness let's take course and shame the devil.

25/09/82

42. Failing Health

O, how people waste
sure so fast,
and drained
of all sap,
of all substance
is this the price we have to pay?
Is this the covenant?
Is there no turn about?
No refund?

When young and agile
O, do we bother to care?
And nimble of limb
do we dare ask these our forms
that we perfume and pollute
of soap and water
of heat combs and nail polish
of obscenities and vices Lord forbid!

Clad in garbs bearing been to manifestations
O, do we take things for granted
and play the master of reality
the star of the movies?
Yet do we take advantage of experiences all
around!
when the time comes?

O, when young and agile
and nimble of limb
do we exercise the faculties

Do we read the meaning
of the skyline, the rainbow bridge
and the Southern Cross,
that scores time
only as seconds and minutes, a journey in a flash!

Soon we cry, we holler
O, youth, how short and deceptively so
is there no reverse gear!
No change? Isn't this a short change?

Count your tears my son
this failing health
is only but the road,
yet much more important than
the destination, Check the milestones.

O, Mother, this note, loud and clear
I am coming home
I've got to reach Chibote Kamuchanga, 122.
Let me esteem and tag onto the road
If this failing health be the means
So be it.

15/03/94
at Kitwe

Note

A message from my late mother.
Died in January 1995.

43. If We Must Die

If she must be born,
give me birth in the maternity -
of the summer,
I've no power to budget -
for the dictates of winter.

For if we must live,
give us a benediction of contentment
in the confines of our poverty -
we've no power to budget -
for the dictates of winter.

And if we must die,
give us a humble death
falling within the means ...
of our humble surroundings ...

A straw mat
and a white sheet
there's no rain here
we fight every day
we die every day.

IF WE MUST DIE

07/09/87
Kalulushi.

44. BORN IN GREY-

Born in grey,
  die in grey.
wailed her grey hair
open the way dear child
she wailed in grey,
death is the beginning of a new order.

We all heard her voice,
we all wondered.

Death in a distant land,
death among distant people.
open the way dear child
she wailed in grey,
her grey hair,

Born in grey,
  die in grey,
death is the beginning of a new order.

and the dead came
and all were excited
the grace of age was sung
and the procession left church
ln a long black pilaster of ants
in black and white
death and a hope
and the last shovelful of earth laid
she stood up and washed her face

Born in grey,
   die in grey.
we all heard her voice
we all heeded
death is the beginning of a new order.

DIE IN GREY.

For Ellings Chomba - Abakalamba besu.

17/05/84

45. The Rain (Tina Infula)

I weep like a lonely
                    spinster,
craving not only belonging
but relief from the pangs of
                    nature
In spite myself the mystery of
                    this existence-
betrays me,
like an orphaned child of five
left to fend like buffaloes in
                    the jungle.
The heart of me weeps
when a look around me reveals
an endless vista of sadness and grief -
                    injustice;
betraying me back to the
little corner where my 'second' mother
heaves,
                    barricaded like a rodent
showered in tears of the heart
she shivers
like a little boy's love
for his sister
                    I cry tears of defiance
I cry out like innocence
for justice.

THE RAIN (TINA INFULA)

16/06/89
for my sister, Schola.

Tina imfula translates- **Beware of the rain,** *in Ichibemba(Zambian language).*

Note:Maintain the shape.

46. **Chitalu**

Why did you do it my dear?
Why didn't you pass by and drop me a lead?
I know not what to make of this
I'm sure you knew neither a thing
I'm left dispossessed
of the only light at the crossroads

And so we journey on; to where?
sure a destination we know now
into a sea of void,
if only to hope, to find you at the gates -
                              - dearest of all
to lead us to our only hope
for happiness eludes us here where you left us
only tears ocean bound.

Queen of a land, a million miles
mother of a place, love so sweet, so sure
yet the only chance within
delude us in no time
tears like oceans deep continue to flow
what fortunes, what love can we claim
when solitude is our only appellation, only call

Life so precious, yet life so plain
a moment I was saying hi!
In a twinkling of an eye, there was no life!

Clouds of promise!

What's the reason for tomorrow
if it's only aptitude in tears, death???
Is there a reason? Existence!
Is it not the only sure thing? Only answer?

We hope to find you at the gates dearest of all
to lead us to our only hope
happiness eludes us here where you left us

Only tears ocean bound

Memories we all have remind us of you

And fresh each day

Rest in peace, love of all

CHITALU

For Chitalu Mwanakatwe, fourth year law student
answered the lords call in
June 1981, hit by a car driven by a drunken youth on
Great east road at the UNZA bus stop.

47. Appointed Time

Is Gods time, appointed time, appropriate time?
Seconds, minutes and hours, 24/7
Every course and every destination,
A full realization of purpose.
                              To count the graces of the
revealed one.
I shall cast myself against the wind
And blow away, right to dire straits
I shall brave the torrents and sing to measure,
A wondrous ascent to Everest
How shall I cry, how shall I mourn M'hango?
To count the graces of the revealed one.
Containers of oceans pacific bound
And seas, black and red, of tears remain dry.
Is this yet another drought?
Or is it in denial conclave,
Waiting upon pilgrim's progress?
                              More, there will be more
questions.
I wonder, I cry tears of dry report
How shall I express this happenstance?
In what mould shall I cast this effigy
This paragon full of life, and laughter fizzled out, out!
How shall I cry, how shall I mourn M'hango?
                              there will be more questions
than answers.
This cast of dignity and duty
Longstanding, painstaking belief and understanding

Embraces of life in all its challenges
Of duty in hand, on hand overcome
In depths 2000 leagues under the sea.
                              there will be more questions
than answers.
To love, to care, to appreciate people;
Going the extra mile
Living life, loving the moment
So, so full of life
Exuding with every possibility and potential
What more can I say?

How shall I mourn Francis?
What shall I call the name, the game!
What report shall I take to account?
To honey, to little daughter and kid brother, to family
No! No sweets shall do, nor statues, nor sweet music.
                              To count the graces of the
revealed one.
To pretend is to harm, was man of the people.
To keep quiet-injustice, his life a report
To document the exploits-cheap-was a priceless
painting
How shall I call to order?
To memories, to posterity, to hope to life.

God's time, Appointed time, Appropriate time.
We count the graces of the revealed one.

APPOINTED TIME.

For the Mhango family.

To the memory and life (celebrated) of Francis M'hango, for and on behalf

Of the Literature in English panel.

Written by Kanyampa M. Manda, in Kalulushi, Chingola- Zambia and Solusi

University – Bulawayo- Zimbabwe.

48. *Fruitless October*

She lay there in sweet abandon
In peace and serenity
In beauty certainty
Radiant with Angelic delight
Her eyes closed
Her mind sure in godly communion
As she sure journeys on ...

We stood there stunned and transfixed
In agony and inconclusion
In hurt certainty
Anguished with dramatic recall
Our eyes red and sore
Our minds in satanic ritual
As we sure journey on ...

She sported the meaningful look of a puzzle
We sported the meaningful look of wonderment
As she lay the deep sleep of the sleeping lions we
          Dare not awaken
As we slept the illusory sleep of dreams horses
          Beggars ride
She spoke the voice of silence
Sweet serene as the undercurrents
We spoke the voice of rage
Questioning the reason why, cursing the
          Lord of this world.

We called her name,
The only answer receive
Her beauty and certainty in promise
Radiant with Angelic delight

Her eyes closed
Her mind sure in godly communion

As she sure journeys on ...

Dust to dust
Ashes to ashes
The sure certainty
The sweetest wine has flowed down
Leaving a scented spirit
On all palms that graced it
And a trail of questions for the reasons why
On this ...

FRUITLESS OCTOBER

by Manda K – for niece PAMELA MWAPE NGUNI
13/10/98

49. Till We Meet Again
(Tribute To A Friend)

Whatever the ills
whatever the misdemeanours
neither of which I want to know!
Kabwe paid his due
in unparalleled vogue
in total
and dearly,
the wicked must get a beating.

09/09/97
for Max Kabwe (A friend)

50. **The Apotheosis: An Ode To Mrs S M Kutty**

Years nostalgic
Already brought
even to this my rawness
and alien culture -
a missing link create ...
And the corridors of Mpelembe
rasps out your absence -
"In a baby come back plea."

Of course time
we cannot start
neither can we hold back
The graves would lie empty,
The stones in wonderment
and indeed no celebrations

Yet anything more suited
to our will deny
our scheme of things,
What directions shall we employ
but inconsistency
In this odyssey of experiences
What name shall we implore.

For your numerous labours'
Lord of the images
whose love and commitment reside

The blue, violet and the yellow rose -
the quintessence
All these things indeed
figure out
the stirring of your heart
the smile and the laughter
the fullness of a kind
the thought for the weak
and weeks on end.

We stare on the vacancy create
Indeed the corridors of Mpelembe
rasps out your absence
we sit and wonder
we'll genuinely remember
with reminiscence
and the poets record ...

The statement pronounced
hard to assess
this picture no one can decipher.
Only time,
and inconsistently so we trudge on
Desperate, but not
full of hopes
If not means alive
of the ground work laid
and the foundations of stone.

Fathered by associations of joys
a love and commitment unparalleled
for the good of the cause
to mould the future
for the various roles ...
come rain or shine

Indeed with a smile
a million miles
and hands a million tons
let this parting shine
and manifest a joyous journey
with the lightness of a feather
the eagle up-high the courts
of heaven
and sharp in eye ...
2 000 leagues under the sea
In pomp and slender
In a halo may ye forever reside
for this apotheosis is complete.

Kanyampa Manda K. M.
16/02/94

51. **The Mystery Of The Paradox**

There's always a caveat
a misty construct over the horizon
a heavy heart and an eclipse over your silver lining
a flip flap of the lower eyelid shadows vision
and dull the spectacle presents the environ.

Anxiety getting the better
and a restlessness of irresolution reigns
and dreams, always of snakes in double tails
and the way is set, the trace stretched out
to the inevitable end.

Yet our infected will, keepeth us from
reaching out onto it.

A head search within reveals not
a call at the crystal ball's draws a blank
and a recoiling inside bears no fruit
efforts to brighten up only transitory
soon the plastic smile harden in a scarecrows grin.

Soon all cosmetic like a fire log
transform into worthless ash
and reality reasserts its supremacy
casting a cloud over your embrace
the mystery of the paradox of life.

Yet our infected will, keepeth us from
reaching onto it.

We learn but little, we heed but not
yet this philosophy repeat every day and death
illusive still
we question, we wonder, we curse
we hope death distant everyday
yet closer still, and dead flowers line cemetery road,

There is always a caveat
yet our infected will keepeth us from
reaching onto it
what about the sweet gift of life
and the sure rest of death?

Yes, the paths of glory lead but to the grave
THE MYSTERY OF THE PARADOX.

February 1998
For Dad, Suffered a stroke on Tuesday
the 30th of December 1997. Was put to rest at
Kansuswa Cemetery in Mufulira
on 2nd January 1998 Forever loving jah.

52. Revelations

(See it in revelations,
you'll find your redemption)
Time has robbed her
of those beautiful years
The song she now sings,
reminiscences,
The only revelation – traces
traces of that, that was a paragon
the scars on her face
recount the sad story
of a perilous life that became
Her presence in local beer places
certifies the rot
Is it society?
Is it the individual?
Is it both?
The ruin has already been
the solution?
Is it my oceans of tears?
Is it my down face?
What shame, Maggie?
Is life so vicious?
Is life unexplainable?
To remain forever a mystery
Is mystery human slavery?
Is slavery perpetual?
Nay! Only mental inconclusion
Clever in essence

But never Maggie
Never to beat the human machine
That which you carry in your head
The only solution
Vigilance,
Resolve and
Conviction
In this struggle for good over evil
for liberation of man the self ...
"see it in revelations,
you will find your redemption."

Mwape Kasongo and MM – 29/04/87
Mwansanga Tavern; where we found her.

THE FOURTH ESTATE

The state of our people
Disturbs me immensely
Walking down compound roads,
A witness of squalor stamps my foot
Taking stock at the playground
A litany of tattered kiddies simulating play
Their diseased tummies barely concealed
Recount the years of denial
Their projections of anguish
Certify the pain felt inside
What choice have I

Our forefathers then, our fathers today
Continue to hew down the stone of transformation
Day in and day out these stone diggers
Inhale heat, dust and smoke
Their silicosis report, chests burnt
Black blood course their laboured veins
Their reward only shacks and wooden hearths
To enhance the temperatures triggered under
There in the bowls of the earth
Their tempers flare up animosity in the back yard
What choice have I?
But to pick up and stone

Cha cha cha was the song then
Transparency, good governance, the anthem today
Both youth and age across the gender divide
To summon and wrestle
To break the chains, the curse, the shame
Of Domination and Damnation
By foreign vultures and local spirits of grand funk
Vampires sucking our blood every day
And freedom came an enabling
environment envisage
We chanted Kwacha!! Ngwee!!
The new dawn, the new deal, the new light

Come mid night that October the flag hoist
An anthem of green, black, red
and orange compose
Kwacha!! Ngwee!!
Songs of patriotism resound
We basked in the sun and sands of independence
And waited for manna to fo llow
In pain and frustration we witness
Naked children of the street return
The blind, the lame, the destitute
Line and malign our corridors of hope

We cry out
where is Uhuru!
What is Uhuru?
What the hell is independence?
One Zambia one nation, still our cry

Dignity and peace, a big question mark
We return to the cold streets, to
shacks, to wooden hearths
Shop corridors our mansions

Street kids, street adults

Vending our bodies!
Frustrated and depressed, mad, ravingly mad
Our brothers and sisters too
Hauling luggages of want, eating
from garbage pan I say
What choice have I?
But to pick up pen and page I cry
out to the Four E'state.

Manda K
October 15 – 2008

The two sides of Love

A basin of water lay before them – man and wife; their faces heavy, with lines reading the sum of the agony and anguish they had suffered in the last week – five days to be exact.

"Dad, I am not feeling well," the phone had said on a Sunday evening.

The report read University teaching Hospital, Monday afternoon, and the personal call message on ZNBC Radio pulled the final curtain on this act – Tuesday, 18:45 hours. Busuma was dead.

Confused and out of sorts, man and wife combed the boundaries of chinsali and took what turned out to be the longest walk in the night. Finally, they found Chungu Wankonde, a renowned witch finder in Sokontwe. This was now past midnight. The Ng'anga by this time had hung his paraphernalia. After listening to their story, the retainer advised them to call the following morning at cockcrow, bearing a white hen, a length of white cloth and some cassava meal. They were advised strictly not to speak to anyone as they returned the following morning and that they should consider it a lost cause should they meet a virgin.

As they waited for the conveyance of the remains of the deceased from Lusaka where she had worked as a teacher, the rites of passage began in earnest at the home of the deceased's parents. Prayers were sung and funeral dirges recited. Tribal cousins were summoned from near and far to come and lead the dirges. At the head of this high-powered delegation of friends and relatives was the head crier, a distant auntie in her late thirties. She eulogized the late's exploits as a village beauty, a family pride and a father's girl. Her history of diligence and upright works was spelt out. This all the more broke the hearts of many and the whole compound roared with wails of all descriptions, that shook the very foundation of the homestead.

Entreaties to the gods of life and laughter, that apparently were the shining guide to Busuma were sought. Notwithstanding these suggestions to love, peace and continuity, the tribal cousins also implored the gods of lightning and thunder to smite one by one, all those whose hands were in the slightest connected to this death. The gods of revenge was called upon to exact justice.

Dressed in his traditional garb of skins and feathers, the witch-finder shouted his routine, in praise of his god-father, now long dead, but whose inheritance he had become to seek guidance.

I am the forest that houses all herbs, clean and dirty, all spirits human and non-human.

I am the sun that shines the day and powers men to their various labours;

The star that lights the night.

The market that stocks all wares and sells them to whoever dares.

I am the water that quenches all thirst and drowns both the innocent and the perpetrators.

I am the road much more important than the destination.

He who beholds me, beholds the truth, the desires of their chest.

Hear me father O! Receive my thanks and praises.

Turning back to the basin, Chung-wa-Nkonde found to his dismay that the water was cloudy and a storm seemed to be raging like on open sea.

"There's a storm in the tea cup," he soliloquized.

He realized all was not well, that a stronger force than he had anticipated was at play. He laughed a guttural laugh. He enjoyed challenging jobs. He muttered a few words of veneration to his god father.

He poured out some beer as a libation and asked his assistant to smoke the medicine room to wad off the evil spirits. M" *...receive my thanks*
and praise father O!
bind with fetters the spirit.
of destruction open the floodgates father O!"

Man and wife were now gripped with fear. They wondered what next. The wife moved closer and clung to her husband and both coughed as the smokescreen took effect. Sooner than later though, all cleared and they could clearly behold the basin in the centre of the room.

Looking at the basin, the rootsman gave out in triumph his traditional guttural laugh.

"I am that I am,"
"I am the natural mystique,
whatever lies hidden I uncover."

And, behold clearly, a face of a man could be seen, plain like an image before a mirror.

"I have your man here," he called out to the couple who were now huddled in the corner of the room.

"Do you wish to behold the face of the man responsible for your tears?"

Yes and no were the answers from the man and wife respectively. As much as they wanted to see for themselves, a deep fear overcame them. They were no longer sure they wanted to be involved that far; indeed they had heard stories of people in similar circumstances transforming into mermaids and mermans.

Realising, they would not dare, Chungu wa Nkonde suggested he covers the face of the perpetrator and only show them the body. To this suggestion, the man consented and for sure he saw the body which he thought he recognized and in his mind's eye, he put a face to it. He withdrew immediately as a lump of anguish almost choked him.

"Three options," offered the witch-finder; to slay the perpetrator immediately, to drive him insane and leave him by the crossroads, and to cause his entire family to perish.

"The last option," they whispered.

"They must all without any exclusion perish," the man intoned, "because the woe they have caused my family will last forever."

Chungu wa Nkonde then took the chicken of black and white and snapped its neck. He also smeared the couple with cassava meal and covered them with a white cloth as the chicken fought for its life.

In the meantime, the medicine man repeated his god father's psalms. As soon as the chicken lay still on the floor, the white screen was removed from the couple. A root was placed in the hands of the man. He was instructed to place it in the palm of the deceased folding it into a boxer's fist. She was to be buried thus.

True to Chungu wa Nkonde's words, they started dying, all manner of death. Death as a result of criminal abortion, death resulting from miscarriage and stillbirths. Accidents, murders, suicide and all excuse of death.

All derivatives of disease and afflictions, short, long term and mysterious beset the clan; and as time went on, the intervals between deaths became shorter and shorter. Soon mourner fatigue set in and neighbours and friends steadily stayed away from what were becoming expensive ventures.

Yet like the rampaging AIDS virus, death continue to take its toll. Blood of family smells, the ancestor said, and so anyone who smelled of that blood ran the risk of sure death. Disquiet resulted in the family as suspicion set in; and the family was not just dying, but quickly sliding into civil war. People started talking, first the neighbors, then friends and acquaintances. The media, both print and electronic, jumped onto the wagon and told this tragic story of a family bedeviled.

It was the pattern and choice of victims that set people thinking. The trend started with the immediate family members – brothers and sisters. Nieces and nephews followed. When the closest of these were done, the endemic set itself upon aunties and cousins. Then the man himself started ailing. His close friends now highly suspicious and worried urged him onto a witch-finder.

Upon examination and scrutiny, it was revealed that the root of the problem was in the family.

"What!" the man gasped and cast eyes of inconclusion upon the man of roots.

"The man who killed your daughter is a relation of yours and the root with which she was buried prescribes death to all members of the clan..."

"Stop!" the man shouted. He couldn't take any more of this; he stood transfixed to the spot; for the next ten minutes, he couldn't find expression. He lost his sense of place and fell in a trance.

In that journey between sanity and insanity, he beheld a large funeral procession. It was a mass burial and his daughter was at the head, directing men where to turn as coffin upon coffin was laid.

She still maintained her stature, as beautiful and as influential. In just a flash, he drifted back to reality.

"How could I have entrusted my life onto the hands of the evil one?" He soliloquised.

"Revenge, wasn't it mine by right? Shouldn't I have avenged the death of my dear one? Yet the innocent blood shed down there. Was I justified to sign the warrant sending so many to death? How could I have loved more, Love, love! And bitterness and revenge and hate and murder! How could that be love? I deserve to die. I couldn't face, I couldn't stand the loss of my daughter. I couldn't brave the fact. How could I forget, how could I forgive? Busuma, my daughter, hear my plea, forgive me, I repent, rest in peace dear one and all the numbers whose blood I now bear. How can I be delivered?"

Thinking this was address to him, the medicine man answered,

"Go and exhume the body of your daughter and take the root off her palm. That will stop the killing."

He didn't wait to listen more. He headed straight for the cemetery where lay his beloved. He sat on the now overgrown mound and started removing the weeds. He cried his head off and exhaustion took effect. He slept the sleep of death.

By the time he was found by the search party the following morning, he was a mad person. Examination by doctors revealed that he had suffered a multiple shock which sent his blood pressure a record high, bursting all veins feeding the brain and so sending blood on to the brain tissue. Two days later, he died and so his number was added to the soaring statistics.

Somebody had to brave the act, to stop these deaths. The medicine man took it upon himself, as his civic responsibility to upraise the grandchildren; for the deaths had now moved to that level. He unfolded the story to them. The grave had to be dug out, the root destroyed.

Realising the shame and braving all tradition and taboo, the grandchildren paid people to open the grave. The question was how were they to identify the palm?

WINNERS NEVER QUIT AND QUITTERS NEVER WIN

He watched the funeral procession leave church yard with a frown. In full pomp and colour, befitting a catholic burial they proceeded. The hearse gleamed in sporty black and white, the air filled with choral music. He heaved inside and tears dropped involuntarily as the gloomy reality took effect. He would not attend the burial of the only woman that meant something to him. They would not allow him.

"How could people be so cruel?" he thought. He followed the procession until the last man disappeared.

Kasuba's mind was boggled in mixed feelings;"To hell with them," he spoke almost aloud, "what is it to me if I don't attend the burial? She's not my sister after all."

That was the proud him. He had walked the world with that kind of inclination. Having been born with stunning features, and given to a rich upbringing, he had always thought himself, the only thing that mattered; what with all the girls in the neighbourhood craving his attention. More so, in school, he was of a mind to quickly grasp and internalise all concepts taught. He made excellent progress skipping a few classes in primary and completing his high school in four years instead of the stipulated five.

The inner voice though, took prominence on this particular day and engaged him into a revealing conversation.

"No my friend," the voice intoned.

"You need to worry. You're not going to transverse this road angering and hurting everyone. Look around you, there is need for you to search within yourself and find cause to feel sorry and apologize," the voice was strong.

"But what have I done," he wondered, "is it wrong to want to pay last respects to a friend?"

With that question, he fell into contemplation. Indeed Eve had been his lover and he had had high regard for her. Being a beauty of the fairies herself, she was jack-pot worth speculating. Many a man, young and old had speculated. He had joined the bee-line and hit the numbers.

For some time, things worked well, with the relationship seemingly stabilizing the haughty young man. Unfortunately, this peace soon came to a close when she announced she had missed her period a consecutive three times. Having been aware of her escapades as a beauty, he had long suspected she was seeing other men and was convinced she had just victimized him. He had left her then.

She gave birth to an ailing child who died within six months. Eve was not the same after she buried her son. She took to brooding and angered at the slightest provocation. Counsel implored her social withdrawal and anti-social behaviour, but to little results. Hers was a combination of grief at the loss of her child and esteem as a result of rejection by Kasuba. The sun had gone down on her. She died six months later. "Could I honestly be blamed for Eve's situation and subsequent death? Could this be the reason why I hurt so much by this denial to attend her funeral?" he thought. Indeed people had whispered that, had he sympathized with her, she could have pulled through; In fact, a representative number of people in the neighbourhood were convinced he was the father of her child. Eve's father had vowed revenge. "Perhaps he was to blame, perhaps he needed to be sorry," Kasuba contemplated. The inner voice was again on hand; "Sorry! You've everything to fear, the death of Eve and her infant earlier could mean AIDS!" He stood spellbound "She had died of AIDS! And the infant before her!" he exclaimed.

"Why have I been so blind, why couldn't I have seen?" Of course, he could not have seen, for he had buried his head in the sand of conceit. For the first time in years, he gave himself a thorough examination. His past life unfolded before him. In this clip, he saw his fast life of women and alcohol. With this came the realization – a lot of his friends and lovers had since died. Those that survived were left with bleeding hearts, and within those hearts he saw accusing fingers pointing at him, vampires stalking for his blood. Fear enveloped him, he shivered "This is the hand of a God!" he told himself. He had hurt so many; he had broken so many hearts. "Lord, whose gonna put the pieces together,"he heaved. "I deserve punishment, like a sheep on the slaughter, Lord God I present myself." With that vow, Kasuba started sliding into sure death. Again, his proud nature took the better of him. He did not consult anybody; neither did he seek medical advice. Like a tortoise, he took to his shell and wallowed in self-pity.

At work people got worried. The exuberance with which he was known to discharge his duties was gone. He seemed to be burdened with heavy weights on his shoulders, yet no one could guess what, neither could they assist. The young man had completely closed all possible inlets.

Like any other serious ailment, emotional sickness could just be as devastating. It was worse for kasuba. He was afflicted not just with AIDS, indeed he had convinced himself he was HIV positive, but by a guilty conscience that dogged him day by day.

He had caused the death of Eve and her infant and she had died without his apology. His sin was final and death was the inevitable end.

Coming from work one day, forlorn and lost in thought, he met Dhaliso. She stared at him in amazement and for some time could not find words. He tried to avoid her but to no avail.

"Is that you! Are you alright kasuba? Why! You've wasted so much, oh my God, I can't believe this. What's the trouble?"

"The lady's entreaties and her strength of character forced him to open up. For the first time he revealed his dilemma and his vow. He poured his whole. He seemed to weaken more. She had to interrupt him to stop the emotion outburst.

"Have you sought medical help?" she asked. "For what dear, can't you see I'm beyond that? No Dhaliso there's only one way for me – death."

She looked at him once again and tears streamed down her face. She was stunned by the this revelation of hopelessness. She burst out: "My God Kasuba, is this really you? Why! You're reasoning like a child. It's not you, the intellectual, the lover boy, to give up on life so! Don't you realize that life is about hope? Man pull yourself together," she implored.

"I've seen people who've suffered worse off fates. I've seen people who've fought HIV! And succeeded and raised families and continued to give hope to others," she heated up with each word said, she continued, "Loneliness, withdrawal, cowardice, rumour mongering, selfishness, is all that makes HIV/AIDS," she paused for a break.

"Man you're a fool; you really insult the integrity of people who looked up to you. Oh, what a coward. I loved you so much, I cried when you left me, I still cry – wasted tears. Life my, friend, is about fighting and winning and often times losing. It is about investing in life and hoping for the better. You've quit even before the fight begins. You've become a quitter, a never winner."

Kasuba meekly took the barrage of censure. He had lost it all. There was no spirit left in him, indeed a sheep for the slaughter. This infuriated Dhaliso. She left him heaving with anger and a growing urgency to find help for the lost soul.

She had walked out on him. She would have nothing to do with a creep, yes that was what he had become, a good for nothing loser. That attack triggered something in him – anger against himself. Of course, he had never been a loser, never a quitter. He had been a winner all along, he had hopped and lived in optimism, he had excelled in school, in social circles, at work. He looked at himself, for sure he had become weak, mind, body and soul. Yet there was no pain anywhere in his body – except his heart. He had heard so much talk about AIDS and its derivatives. He didn't seem to have any such clues. The more he examined himself, the more Dhaliso's words rang true:

"You're a fool."

There was nothing wrong with him, but a feeble mind and a dirty conscience and a dirty humanity; And all he had tried to live in order to atone himself of Eve's death, was to carry single handedly humanity's sin, that of negative thinking and living on his shoulders. It was that kind of living that had nurtured AIDS and made it pandemic, it had thus eaten at his heart and drained him of almost all sap. He had found the cure. The rot in his mind, the foolish pride, the selfishness, the guilty conscience, the loneliness must be routed out.

He rushed to Dhaliso's place shouting 'Eureka'.

THE DREAM OF REASON

The scene is the arid lands of the far direction, the reality, a smoke screen, the night before the final onslaught. The divine King Manor fetes his gallants.

"We've gone this far, we're going all the way, tomorrow, at half-mast, the Camerian Fowl must fly. We shall rise and sing in salute of the Fowl of the Castle ...!"

And six times, facing the holy massif, up and down they went in godly communion. Names were called out and rings of gold, bearing the Fowl of the Castle graced their ring fingers. Each gave the holy salute.

'God is mighty' and in unison, they rhymed 'For better, for worse, for the sake of our beloved de-parted' and the twenty six guns reverberated in reverent salute.

As the Cannon sound subsided, the divine commander, infuriated perhaps by the blasts, rose breaking all ritual, bid punishment to all traitors.

'He who looks down, 'he intoned, 'is the enemy that dogs our ranks, consign them to earth' came the report from the lieutenants. A hoard of ill clad men and women – manifesting signs of dejection presented themselves before his majesty, begging for mercy without speaking. On deaf ears fell their unspoken entreaty.

As these were lined up, to the firing squad their appellations were written.

The report of the first shots sent his majesty reeling in a trance. For a time, all went mute, devoid of all movement as his majesty recoiled in meditation. A procession appeared before him. In pomp and colour, they presented before him an overflow of oil barrels on a silver platter, leading the procession, the palace jester sang:

'God is mighty, even to the weak'.

This vision in a mirage of change, gave King Manor a head of a creature, with blood oozing from all outlets, multiplying each time in myriad – subtleties.

The blast is heard amid shouts:

'Weakness, Treachery, Treason, Death!'

Cannon fire is sound to close the ceremony; with it, three green stars float in Manor's head. He sees the mother Fowl in mound, spreading its arms seemingly to recapture its runaway children.

II

King Manor enjoyed working the early hours. At the struck of 2 a.m., he awoke but to a dream. Vivid, clear. He is back in his mothers' womb – a foetus, bidding the Creator to hasten his passage.

'I'm the last hope, let me go save fatherland'.

'No!, his mother protests, 'There is war, there is famine out there, how many more shall I lose!' "Mother, my poor brothers and sisters are out there, suffering, what comfort is that for us, me! Somebody must rise, sacrifice and restore sanity, somebody, I present myself, mother, I must go. Grant leave, let me go"

Leaders are born, made! Rebels are born, circumstances present, defusing in situational leadership!

III

A rebel is born and an army rose against the will of mother reason. In his rage, he multiplies into a million foetuses, committing his mother into induced labour.

IV

At heaven's gate stands the Creator with a bag of fates. It is again the king's jester with the same message.

'God is mighty, even to the weak'.

Straight into the raging fires of enemy bombardment. Into this conflagration surge the fighting foetuses, turning instantly into aliens of smoke and marshy ash, defeated even as they release their lethal report.

The victors tossed, but amid coughs and a strange feeling.

V

At a Cenotaph in Cameria stood a lone woman, her eyes heavy. The inscription read:

'TO THE UNKNOWN SOLDIERS'

Up sky hovered the Camerian Fowl, flying low, like in half mast and somewhere, the song 'Vietnam' could be heard.

The Taj Mahal.

Mutinta: (*Walking towards front stage as the curtains unfold*) I will ride the Southern Cross like the last mile.

Chorus: (*in unison*) Sitting at my study table, burning the midnight lamp –my crystal ball, what do I see.

Mutinta: (*joining in*) indeed the load-star on that Indian Horizon-The Taj Mahal.

Kakoma: (*Sarcastically*) that's how desperate they get, arms out stretched, soup-bowls they present at street corners for alms. No alms for Sunday – out, out of my way!

Mutinta: (*ignoring*) I will give thanks and praises. On this altar of brown and blue, I present myself as burnt offerings of gratitude. In this milky-way, what do I see.

Kakoma: (*Interrupts*) only shooting stars in a dead sky, that's all. (*To the audience*) They pray, and pray, these idle minds – fortune seekers and wait for miracles – gunning for gold, reaping where they never sowed – shoot!

Mumbi: (*Bible in hand, in prayerful poise*) Lord, give me the land of milk and honey.

Kakoma: (*Laughing*) Building castles in the air, that's their Taj Mahal. Shoot!

Mumbi: (*Facing the sky*) A Street lined up with sky-scrapers.

Kakoma: (*Laughing*) a street in New York! In Dubai! A concrete jungle! Can you manage one? (*Challenging Mumbi*) O! I fear, these will soon come tumbling down, killing the innocent ones, look at that Cathedral disaster in West Africa, empty prophesies!– back where we started – streets lined up with beggars – disaster funds, I see another BAND AID, soup bowls, another Tsunami.

Mutinta: (*Concerned, calls Matimba and Kakoma*) come here my friends. Look here, you seem to have forgotten who I am, were we started, we sat on the same desk, remember!

Kakoma &
Matimba: (*together laughing, protesting*) you! Forget you! Did we know you in the first place? Now you have a voice!

Mutinta: (*In a reconciliatory tone*) calm down friends. Why the hot blood –jealousy and hate is blinding you, you are misdirecting yourselves – you are young, energetic- the sky is the limit. You need to focus on the matter, get back on the ground and see things as they really stand. You see these scholarships....

Kakoma: (*agitated*) Scholarships my foot! Who is talking about scholarships here?

Matimba: (*Cutting in*) Come to think of it, how did we miss out on these? How come only dreamers, Compound dross! Good for nothings like you....

Mutinta: (*Thoughtfully*) Now, that's more like it. Matimba lets sober up – Yes, I might not have been the coolest guy on the block, I might have missed out on the leisure trip, but that's history now. Look, the whole thing is about scholarship, hard work and commitment to a cause – Yes it is about dreams.

Chorus: (*cutting in*) A focus about the future, about what I want to become, 10 years from now – a surgeon helping Zambia

out of this theatre of poverty and disease
Yes I am a dreamer for mother Zambia.

Mutinta: (*echoing*) it is about attitude,
gratitude to our parents,
                    for being there for us, for
urging us on, each day.
                    What about our teachers?
The ever green team
That provided knowledge and counsel, Over
and above all,
Konkola Copper Mines Plc. For the wonderful
support
                    For the beautiful schools,
endowing them with all the requisites,
                    providing an atmosphere for
scholarship.

Chorus: Thank you KCM
                    Thank you CEO for this life
line to Zambia
                    Education is the future
                    You couldn't have empowered
us more
                    We will not let you down
                    We pledge hard work
                    That's our big thank you
                    We present ourselves as burnt
offerings
                    On this altar of brown and blue,

Thank you, KCM

Matimba &
Kakoma: (in contemplation) that's cool, focus, scholarship! Attitude. We lacked

'gratitude, we missed the boat.

Matimba: But definitely not the plane, the sky is our starting point, let's get on board, on board!

Kakoma &
Matimba :   (together) we will get on board, we will fast track, we will hit the destination- the `Taj Mahal.

Chorus: (*cutting in*) A focus about the future, about what I will become, 10 years from now – a surgeon helping Zambia out of this theatre of poverty and disease Yes I am a dreamer for mother Zambia.

Basic Poetry Literary Elements

1. **Simile** – a comparison of two unlike things using 'like' or 'as'. Example:

"Some things never change; they are like the moon and stars.

As round as the Copernicus construct defying all odds.

2. **Metaphor** – a comparison of two unlike things without using like or as:

"When it comes to hard work, she's George Orwell's Boxer."

3. **Personification** – an inanimate object is given human like characteristic:

"The **confused lake beat up the dugout canoe killing all the passengers.**

4. **Hyperbole** – a great exaggeration:

When it comes to food, she commands the appetite of a thousand pigs.

5. **Alliteration** –at the beginning of words, there is a repetition of consonant sounds. In the poem

THE POWER OF LOVE:

Conflagration to **consume, Love** paves and **lights** the way, **love sings** the **song** of **life.**

6. **Repetition** – The repetition of the same word or phrase throughout a work or a section of a work

to achieve effect or to emphasise. In the poem WHISPERING WINDS AND SANDS OF TIME, the phrase-**The whispering winds and sands of time** is repeated for effect. Repetition also introduces **rhythm,** the musical effect to a piece of poetry.

7. **Onomatopoeia** – words that sound like the name of the word: In the heat of the October sun, the **bees buzzed** by the main gate and somewhere by the ant hill a snake **hissed.**

8. **Allusion** – A casual reference to a famous historical or literary figure or event, in the poem *These young lovers,* there is reference to Robin Hood, reference to Lady Diana – Paparazzi, and back in ham Palace, the Holy Bible in the bread of life, and the fall of the Soviet Union in the mention of Perestroika.

9. Persona – Character of figurative disguise /guise that a writer/poet/singer uses as he performs/writes. The persona can also represent the voice in a poem/ work of art.

10. **Rhyme** – The repetition of closely related sounds in the syllables of different words especially at the end of lines e.g. Sweeter/ bitter, ever/never.